Victor DiGenti, Author of the *Windrusher Trilogy*, "Mary Ann Bator-Gray's delightful tale is sure to delight both the young and the young at heart. Jaden's adventures with Keelee and his four-legged friends in search of the lost toys carries the reader on an adventure they will long remember."

Maggie Carter-de Vries, Author of *Amelia's Secrets* and *Ghosts of Amelia and Other Tales*, "*Jaden and the Weejum* is delightful! A beautifully spun tale of the love between our four-legged friends and those who care for them."

Best Wishes
Mary Ann Bator-Gray
2011

Jaden and the Weejum

A Cats Angels' Adventure

By

Mary Ann Bator-Gray

"One for all and all for the love of cats," Lydia's chant as the matriarch of the feline adventurers.

This book is dedicated to Beth Hackney, founder and president of Cats Angels, to the board of directors, and to all the volunteers who work hard to create a better environment for our four legged buddies, both feline and canine.

The story is also dedicated to my wonderful grand daughter, Jaden, who is an occasional Cats Angel and my inspiration.

ACKNOWLEDGEMENTS

The author would like to thank all of the people who provided permission to use their photographs in this book. A special thanks to Jan Cote-Merow and Evelyn C. McDonald for their editorial comments.

CHAPTER ONE

The Happening

My knees and my elbows hurt as I crawled into bed. When I thought about falling in front of my friend, Marcy, today, all clumsy and stupid, my face got hot all over again. And as if that wasn't bad enough, the weird things that happened later left my head spinning.

Something woke me up. As I opened my eyes, the moonlight made silver strings on the floor through the blinds on my window. Lifting my head from the pillow, I heard a little sound. Was it coming from my playroom? I lay still, watching the shadows in my room, waiting. It was quiet now.

I glanced at my fairy nightlight, glowing from a plug in the wall. Brushing my long, brown hair away from my face, I squinted, trying to see in the dim light. Then deciding I must have been wrong about the noise, I pulled my soft, purple quilt up to my chin and shut my eyes again.

"Jaden, wake up. Please help me." The voice was a whisper, only inches from my ear. I turned my head and jolted up. My nose bumped into something warm—skin?

Rubbing my eyes, I tried to chase away what I thought was a dream, but it wasn't. I stammered, "What? Who are you, and..." I gasped. "What are you?"

I peered into large, dark brown eyes then lifted my body to rest on my elbows. "Ouch!" They still burned. Using my heels, I inched back against my headboard to get farther away from the creature. Yet, he was cute...not really scary, with a round face, and a tiny nose and chin. Like a kid, but those ears? They were big and the tops folded over like a floppy-eared rabbit.

I raised my fist to my mouth to stop a giggle. Laughing at him would be rude. His clothes were funny too. The small person stepped away from my bed. His body was similar to the boys in my third grade class, but he was only two feet tall. This must be a dream. I rubbed my eyes again.

"My name is Keelee, and I'm a Weejum. My people rescue lost dolls among other treasures. I heard yours crying and want to help you find her."

"I must have eaten too much ice cream last night. That's why I'm seeing you. My porcelain doll is in my Victorian dollhouse in the playroom." I lied, wanting him to go away. "Besides, toys don't cry."

"If they're scared they do." His eyes got big. "She's gone. Come see for yourself."

I slid from my bed, stepped through the bathroom, and shivered when my bare feet touched the cold tiles. Turning on the light in the next room, I looked over my favorite place. Everything seemed as it should be—well, almost. A few games were scattered across the floor, making the room look a bit messy. The pictures of ballet dancers in pink fluffy skirts on my walls were straight. My Barbie dolls and books still set neatly on shelves.

Keelee stood by the low table that held the dollhouse. He opened the door, scratching the edge across its wide porch. "Come see; hurry. There's not much time."

I glanced at the white scalloped trim and yellow shutters with hearts in them. A big lump stuck in my throat because I already knew my toys weren't there. The stool behind the ivory piano in the living room was empty, so was the lace canopy bed in another room. A curly haired doll wearing a pink flowered dress and a white pinafore was nowhere to be seen. I touched the white, lacy baby carriage next to the porch where her kitten, Snowy, usually napped. That was empty too.

Keelee placed on hand on his hip. "See? She's missing. Are you going to help me find her or not?"

Tears filled my eyes. "Grandma gave me her very own doll, kitten, and dollhouse for my birthday. They're old and she said to take good care of them."

I slumped to the carpet and lowered my head, starting to feel sick to my stomach. My friend, Marcy, insisted I take Melanie and Snowy with us on our bike ride. I didn't want to make her angry with me. That's when I must have lost them.

"Shush." Keelee placed his finger against his lips. "I can hear Melanie. I can't do this alone."

"I can't hear a thing. What's she saying?" My answer sounded clear in the quiet room, but I couldn't believe I was speaking to what had to be an imaginary creature.

Keelee closed his eyes and looked like he was thinking hard. "Her voice is very soft and I hear water splashing. Sounds like she's saying dirt and sand are everywhere. She's cold. Please come find her."

I was still deciding if I believed him when I heard a rattle at the window. Keelee sprinted to the pane and shoved it up. "Bout time you guys got here!"

My heart began pounding so loud I thought everyone could hear it. Four cats leaped onto the blue carpet, bringing the scent of pine trees with them. They scratched the needles from their fur with their back paws. Two of them looked like they wore tuxedoes with white shirts and the other two were totally black.

The first one to speak looked familiar; in fact they all did. My grandmother helps take care of the animals at Cats Angels, a local rescue center. Sometimes I go with her.

"Had trouble resetting the security alarm at the center when we sneaked out, mon ami." One cat's head cocked to the side and I noticed his clipped ear.

"My gosh, you're DT and you can talk." My voice was squeaky and I'm sure my eyes were bigger than full moons.

"Only when Weejums are around. Name's really d'Artagnan. Big Blackie, Slinky, and Shakespeare are my musketeers."

"Wow! You know Keelee?"

He bowed then straightened. "We help him all the time. Great adventures to tell mes amis back at the shelter."

I recognized the French words, mon ami, which means my friend, from cartoons and books I'd read. "Are you from France?"

DT uttered a cat like chuckle. "No, Fernandina Beach, Florida, but d'Artagnan was French. I try to be like my hero when I'm with the Weejums."

"Oh." I was still trying to catch my breath. My head felt all fuzzy inside when a new door appeared on the wall. Shiny jewels glittered, and light bounced off the ceiling from the sparkling portal. I glanced at the Weejum. The various colors matched his clothes, bright green like his pants, orange as his suspenders. He wore a red shirt with buttons of different sizes, some with small gems much like the door. Keelee tapped his foot with impatience. High-topped yellow sneakers covered his feet, and red and white striped socks scrunched

3

over the tops.

My knees began to wobble. This was all so strange. "Why do you need my help?" I tucked strands of hair behind my ear and fingered my barrette like I usually do when I'm nervous.

Keelee stretched out his arm and his fingers. "See, can't reach the doorknob. Besides, Melanie and Snowy belong to you."

The cats sat at attention like little soldiers, tails wrapped around them. "Don't look at us, mon ami. Haven't mastered round knobs yet, only levers."

"But my daddy and mommy will be worried if I'm not here in the morning."

Keelee smiled. "You will be. I promise. Time moves very slowly in my world."

***

CHAPTER TWO

The Land with no Name

I stared at the dazzling door in my playroom for a few seconds, then made my decision. As I wrapped my fingers around the doorknob, the metal felt cool in my palm. It turned easily, but my hand shook. Slowly, I pulled open the door.

"Wow!" I gasped. Millions of colored twinkle lights filled the air around a smooth, checkered, rock path.

"Ready?" Keelee grabbed my hand and began running through the opening without waiting for my reply.

DT and Big Blackie dashed to our side, long tails out straight, while Slinky and Shakespeare followed close behind. My legs pumped and the lights raced past. Then the path disappeared before my eyes, and I jolted to a stop.

"It's fine. It always does this. We'll be there soon," Keelee said with a big grin.

"Oh my gosh!" I squealed as the Weejum yanked me into motion again. With the ground beneath my feet turning invisible, my stomach started to do summersaults.

Ahead a patch of blue appeared beyond the lights, sky...and white clouds. Where the path ended, a green haze began. I held my breath. Keelee and the cats were running straight for it, pulling me with them. Then the misty stuff became trees and grass. I stumbled forward and landed on my bottom in a meadow covered with Texas blue bells.

"I can't believe this," I whispered.

I looked around, then down, as my hand touched the soft cloth of a red shirt and green pants. What happened to my nightgown? Something tickled the back of my neck. I

5

reached up and felt a ponytail held together by my barrette.

"Where are we? Does this place have a name?"

"Nope, call it what ever you want to. The portal changes your clothes if you're curious."

"Hmmm." I wrinkled my nose. "It's not night time here."

"Day and night are reversed and time is much slower."

"What do we do now, Keelee?"

"Follow the path through the woods. We'll go to my village first."

The cats stretched and sharpened their claws, scratching the bristly grass, then took the lead. In a short while, the tall pine trees ended at a large, flat field. Row after row of tiny houses made circles in the open space. In the center, a large bell hung from wooden posts and a hammer dangled from a rope next to it. The small buildings with pointed roofs and crooked doors and windows, looked like my crayon drawings from two years ago. As I watched, the smoke from chimneys drifted upward in lazy curls. The smell of chocolate chip cookies filled my nose.

Keelee strolled to the bell and swung the hammer. Placing my hands on my ears, I winced. Doors clattered open and hundreds of Weejums ran towards us.

"You all look alike, almost," I whispered. My eyes widened. All but the hair and eye color were the same. Some of them had braids and I guessed they were girls. Soon, purple baseball hats with different painted letters made a polka dot pattern on the town square.

"Welcome to Nowhere." A boy with a smiling face and a round belly stepped from the crowd. He extended his palm. "Name's Winslow."

I shook his hand. His cap had a W while Keelee's had a K. I clasped the bill of my cap and took it off of my head. Sure enough, a white letter J set in the middle. Tiny caps set backwards on the heads of the cats, but theirs had holes for their ears. A red feather stuck up from the back of DT's.

"We need supplies. We're off to find Melanie and Snowy," Keelee said.

Winslow nodded. "Already knew they were missing. We'll get what you need."

After the little people darted away, Keelee showed me the town. "What's in there?" I stopped in front of a large building with walls of uneven length and a rickety roof.

"Warehouse for spare parts." He opened a creaking door.

The cats whizzed past, sounding like a heard of elephants on the wood planks of the floor. I peered through the cobwebs and the faint light. Windows surrounded the large space, but they were high on the walls. The room was filled with stacks of broken toys: wheels of all sizes, Barbie clothes, shoes, brushes and other assorted doll things, kite tails, paddles without balls and balls without paddles, Lego blocks...

I placed my hand on my mouth. "Geez! Where did you get all this stuff?"

"Comes here when things get lost and no one cares. Some kids don't. But when someone does, like you, we help them find their belongings. Can even fix 'em if they get broken while they're missing." His big eyes twinkled and he puffed out his chest.

"No mice, mes amis." DT flashed us a big, white fanged smile.

I shuddered glad to hear the news. Keelee scampered to the edge of the smallest pile and began sifting through it. "So far, there's no dolls or kittens. We'd better get going."

I followed him back to the town square. Two backpacks were waiting for us. It was easy to tell by the size which one was mine. I picked it up and shoved my arms through the straps. Keelee pointed to an opening in the woods on the other side of town. Weejums lined the trail, waiting for us.

"Wish you well." They all shouted and waved.

"Thank you." I trotted past with my gang.

As we made our way into the forest, birds and crickets chirped. The sun shone brightly through the tops of the trees. Soon the path became rocky and rose steeply upward. As we climbed, the air became colder. The sky darkened. Shivering, I stepped from the woods into an area of snow-covered hills.

I rubbed my hands together. "What now?"

"Don't know. Every adventure is new. Guess we'll have to move forward and see what happens."

"Can't we go back to your village?"

"Not without Melanie and Snowy. We can only move forward after you choose our path, never backwards."

"Me?" I didn't like that idea. "But I'm cold." I moaned, glancing over my shoulder at the thick trees. The path was gone and the bushes near the ground too thick to get through.

Keelee sat on a rock, surrounded by black cats, and slipped his bag from his shoulders. "Whatcha need is in your backpack. Take a look."

"Really?" I opened the zipper, reached inside, and felt

7

something soft and warm. Smiling, I pulled out a pink hooded jacket. "Wow! How does the bag know what we need?" I slipped on the coat. There were mittens in the pockets too.

"You ask too many questions." His mouth formed a little pout.

"And you don't have many answers."

He bit his bottom lip and gave me a lopsided grin. I giggled at the silly face he made. Then my mouth dropped open. A giant white cloud seemed to fall out of the sky. It was rolling towards us—fast. A blizzard, speedier than the eighteen wheel trucks I saw on the freeways at home.

Keelee saw it too. His eyes got big. He yelled over the oncoming thunder, "The Whities! They'll cover us with snow and we won't be able to breathe. We gotta hide."

I looked around. "Over there, fallen logs, hurry!" I shouted.

The cats pushed back their ears and dashed forward. Grabbing Keelee's hand, I ran for cover. The ground was slippery. My feet slid out from under me and my behind hit the snow. The awful rumble was getting louder. "Come on." I struggled to my feet, and reached for Keelee's hand again. Black paws, some with white toes tossed the earth beneath the logs into the air.

"Get a move on, you two." Big Blackie shouted over his shoulder.

We reached the pile of wood and clawed a space beneath the timbers next to our furry friends. It was only large enough to squeeze in our bodies. Now the sound was a deafening roar. We all ducked our heads and covered our ears.

Swooshes, whops, and whumps sounded over our heads. Screeching, howling and pitiful sobs followed. Clearing the snow from my face with my mittens, I lifted my head and peeked at the disaster. Snowmen or snow people parts, I couldn't be sure which, were everywhere. Odd shaped balls of many sizes, broken twigs that used to be arms, and chunks of coal, once eyes and mouths, littered the ground. But something else got my attention. Near one of the snowy heads, a pink-flowered piece of wet cloth shimmered. It was a part of Melanie's dress.

"Are you okay?" Keelee whispered in my ear.

"Yes, but look over there. I'm sure it belonged to my doll. Wonder how it got there and if the Whities know anything about it?"

"We can ask them, but we need a plan. They're going to

be mighty upset, blaming us for what happened."

"But it wasn't our fault." My eyebrows bunched together and my lips pressed into a tight line.

"Doesn't matter. They aren't very smart—ice instead of brains."

"Okay. How about we put them back together? That'll make them happy, won't it? We can pick up the coal, find new twigs for their arms..." My face brightened, then the scowl returned. "Oh no, their black, top hats are smashed flat."

"My turn to look in my backpack." Keelee grinned, pulling out a stack of purple baseball caps like the one he was wearing minus the initial. "Told ya. The bags always have what we need."

"Okay; let's get to work." I crawled out from under the logs.

The cats scampered into the woods. Keelee and I rolled fresh snow onto the balls we found and stacked them three high. I grunted from the hard work. The balls making up some of the bellies were heavy. Four cats looked like black lightening as they whizzed back and forth from the woods, carrying twigs and coal in their teeth. When there were several rows of snow people, I stood back to admire our work. The creatures were still and silent.

"Blimey, the cat's got their tongues." Shakespeare snickered, nodding at the Whities and shaking the icicles from his thick, long fur.

"Don't look at me, I didn't do it." Slinky sauntered up, stuck his chin forward, and twitched his whiskers.

Seeing their fallen brothers, the creatures we'd put together began to cry. We hurried. As we fixed the rest of the snow people, the once horrible sobbing turned to soft whimpers. The Whities turned their heads admiring each other. Finally shouts of praise filled the air. Sticks clapped together. I held my ears. Snow people sure were loud.

Then I trudged through the snow to where the cloth lay and picked it up. When the celebrating died down I asked, "Where did this come from?" The pretty material fluttered in the breeze as I held it in my fingers.

"Found it at the fork in the road." It was the smallest of the snow clan that answered.

Keelee whispered in my ear. "Couldn't have been there long, not much ice on it." He stepped closer to the little snow person. "Will you show us where that is?"

"Sure." The snow creature turned with a swish and waddled up the hill. Everyone followed and stopped when the ground became flat. "Found it right here." He bounced up and down on his round bottom.

"So where do you think it came from?" I asked.

His twiggy arms pointed in two directions. One continued up the mountain, the other led to a new trail in the woods that seemed to go downward.

I frowned in confusion. "What's in either direction?"

"Up there's the castle of the three headed bird. The other path goes to the red valley. Never been that far. Don't know what's there."

I looked at the nodding heads of the snow people and bit my bottom lip. That's all the help we would get. I glanced at Keelee.

He tilted his head. "You have to choose."

"Why me?"

"Your toys."

***

If Jaden chooses to go to the castle, continue on the next page, Chapter Three-A. If she picks the red valley, turn to page eighteen, Chapter Three-B.

CHAPTER THREE-A

Three Headed Bird

I stared at the rocky trail leading upward with a frown. "It's scary. Look how skinny it is and how close it gets to the edge of the mountain."

Keelee's eyes narrowed, peering into the distance. "We'll have to go slow and be very careful."

We started the journey. Soon a heavy mist filled the air. It was hard to see through it, but at least it wasn't cold. The cats scampered ahead, their tails held high. I grabbed Keelee's hand as he walked behind me, then placed my other hand on the scratchy, stone wall. The path curved in and out. Old tree branches and stumps stuck out from the mountainside.

As I climbed over a snarled chunk of wood, I looked around. My heart pounded in my chest. The valley below seemed very far down. I inched forward. My sneaker bumped into something hard, a low pile of rocks. I stumbled. One of the larger boulders loosened and went tumbling over the edge with a rumble. A chunk of the path went with it. Keelee tottered over the hole that formed in the path.

"Hurry; jump!" I screamed with my eyes glued to the dangerous opening in front of him.

He filled his round cheeks with air and leaped. His feet slid on the rocky soil when he landed on my side of the hole. I winced in fear he might fall backward into the crack. His small body tottered on the edge. Stretching my arm, trying not to look down, I grabbed onto his shirt and tugged. He fell forward on top of me.

"Gee, thanks." Keelee gasped, holding his hand over his heart.

11

"No problem." I barely got out the words since I was breathing hard too. I leaned my head and shoulders against the mountain. Then I bent my knees and let my body slide until my behind thumped the ground. DT and his gang wandered back to us.

Slinky cocked his head. "Hey dudes, what's up?"

DT peered into the hole then looked at Keelee and me. "Broke the trail. Did you eat too many crêpes?"

Shakespeare sat on his big rump next to DT. "Bloody good show, mates."

"Forgetaboutit," Big Blackie grumbled.

"Not funny, guys. We've got a problem." Keelee sank beside me. "We can go higher. What do you want to do, Jaden?" He pointed to the ledge above our heads.

"Is it safer up there?" I asked.

"Don't know, but this way isn't." He nodded at the path ahead. Large rocks made the way even scarier than it was before.

I stared at the cliff above not wanting to make a decision. "Geez, guys, I must have picked the wrong path." I hung my head.

Keelee patted my shoulder. "The other one could have been worse."

"Oh." It was nice of him to say that, but I wasn't feeling better. Then I spotted a bunch of short ledges and smiled. "I see some steps. Follow me."

I climbed then winced, tossing my body onto the hard shelf. At least this was wider than the lower trail. After we hiked a while I moaned, "Let's rest. I'm thirsty."

Sitting with my legs stretched out in front of me, I peeked into my backpack and grinned. I wrapped my fingers around a cool bottle of water and a bowl. The pack was empty again like it was after I pulled out my jacket.

Sharing the drink with Keelee and our furry friends, I looked around. The mist began to clear. We were almost at the top of the mountain, yet I didn't see a castle. Ahead was a rock bridge leading to a large flat space. But the bridge was thin in places. Could it hold our weight? My eyebrows pinched together.

"Ready?" Keelee asked, bouncing to his feet as if nothing was wrong.

"Isn't there another way? That thing looks ready to break."

"Nope. And the path behind us is already gone."

We were sitting a few inches from the edge of the

mountain. Only air filled the space where the path used to be. I trembled, crawled forward, then stood. Stepping onto the bridge, my knees began to wobble. There was nothing to hold onto. Half way across I heard a horrible rumble and dozens of loud crackling sounds. The bridge began to sway. I screamed.

"Yowzer!" Slinky screeched.

"Run. Don't look down, and don't look back." Keelee's little feet kicked up dust as he sprinted forward.

He grabbed my hand and pulled me with him. The cats' bodies stretched like black rubber bands, their claws scraping the stone. The thunder continued. Chunks of rock fell from the bridge. The gritty dirt in the air tasted yucky. My heart pounded in my chest. There was nothing beneath my feet. Tears filled my eyes. Arms waving, I was tumbling through the air…spiraling down.

"Keelee!" I yelled as my body jerked upward, and my jacket zipper pinched my throat. I was no longer falling. Glancing over my shoulder, I saw a huge black eye and black feathers. I gulped. A black bird at least five times my size held me in its beak and was flying to the top of the mountain.

Three Headed Bird

Adapted from a Photo of a Raven by Ingrid Taylar Found at Wikipedia.org

As I watched, another head appeared holding Keelee then another—the three headed bird. My pulse began to thump wildly. Where was it taking us? What would the bird do when it got to where ever it was going? And what happened to DT and the musketeers? I was too scared to cry.

"Holy creepers!" I screeched as my body was dumped into something. I didn't know what. Thin sticks poked my bottom and made crunchy sounds when I moved.

"Yikes!" Keelee yelled, landing next me.

I peeked out through a pile of feathers and sneezed. It was a huge nest. Three giant ravens flew down and perched on the edge.

"This isn't a three-headed bird after all. They only fly close together." My voice was low so the creatures wouldn't hear.

"Told you snow people weren't very bright. This isn't a castle either." Keelee sat on his heels. One of the birds hopped closer. "What do you want with us? Weejums and humans taste awful. We don't make a good dinner."

Oh no, dinner? A dark head bobbed several times as if considering the idea. I shivered.

Another bird tossed his head back and his chest began to bounce. "Eat you? Yuk, yuk, yuk."

Could that be a laugh? I bit my lip, hoping it was, and then glanced at Keelee.

"We only eat berries," the second bird said. "You no berry. Can't fool me. Yuk, yuk."

"What you do here? Not come for our treasures?" The third raven spread his wings and flapped them fast. He began to squawk.

I inched closer to Keelee. "We won't take anything. We're looking for a lost doll and a kitten. Have you seen them?"

"What's a doll?"

"Kitten? That a berry?"

"Yuk, yuk."

"This is hopeless. They're worse than the snow people." Keelee scratched his head.

I felt around the nest for my backpack. My fingers grasped something soft. Lifting my hand, my eyes became huge. It was a piece of lacy, white cloth from Melanie's pinafore. It had to be. I searched again and found strands of pink, satin ribbons with tiny silk flowers like those from the wreath around Snowy's neck.

"Look, Keelee," I said, excitement bubbling in my chest.

"These are from my toys. We have to get the birds to tell us where they found them."

"Let's find our packs. There must be something in them to help us," he whispered.

I twisted and turned, feeling around the nest again. Keelee did the same thing.

"Got it." I smiled.

"Me too."

I reached into my bag and pulled out a shiny object. My jaw dropped. "I've got a mirror with a gold frame and handle."

Keelee grinned and opened his palm. It was a beautiful marble, almost as big as his fist. Rainbow colors swirled on its pearly surface. He stood in the nest and pushed back his shoulders. His voice was deeper than I'd ever heard it. "I have a new treasure for you if you show us where you found these." He dangled the cloth and ribbons with one hand and clutched the marble in the other, spreading his fingers so the birds could see the shine.

"Oooh. Gimmee." All three birds cawed and jumped forward. Keelee thrust his fist behind his back.

"Show them the mirror, but don't let them snatch it," he whispered.

I held it out with my fingers wrapped tightly around the handle. "What are we going to do? There are three birds and the pack only gave us two treasures. You said it would give us what we need."

"It did. What's in your hair?" He smiled looking at me.

I touched my head and giggled. "A barrette. Of course, it's metal and shiny." I unclipped the hairpiece and held it in my palm.

The birds screeched and fluttered their wings. I saw Keelee tuck the cloth and ribbons into his pants pocket before he was snatched into the air. My feet left the nest at the same time, and then the birds were soaring off the top of the mountain. The air whipped my face. Soon, the mountain disappeared into the clouds. I squeezed my eyes shut and held my breath.

A few minutes later, we were dumped onto a large pile of sand, landing on our backsides. The three ravens stood where two paths joined in a "V", each leading in a different direction. One bird scratched the white powder with his claw and uncovered another pink ribbon.

"Gimmee shinnies," a second bird said.

"Me too," the third bird crowed.

Keelee and I placed the three treasures on the sand. The birds quickly grasped them in their beaks. Then large black wings filled the air. "Yuk, yuk, yuk," they called as they flew away.

I looked at Keelee. "You sure have strange creatures in your world."

"No more than you have in yours." Keelee pocketed the ribbon.

"What do you mean?"

Keelee shuffled his feet. "How about large steel birds without feathers. A little boy lost one of those once."

"You mean airplanes?"

"If that's what you call 'em.'"

I pursed my lips. "I guess it depends on what you're used to, whether you think something is weird or not."

"Yep." Keelee gave me a lopsided grin.

I stood and looked around. We were on a large sand dune where sea grass grew in patches. Behind me was the ocean, bringing the scent of salty air. At least it looked like it. Waves crashed onto the beach. Pelicans dove into the water and came out with fish flopping in their bills. White gulls glided like kites overhead. Then I heard a rustle and four whiskered faces peeked out from a tangle of vines.

I breathed a sigh of relief. "What happened to you guys?"

"Birds." DT pressed his paw to his lips and made a kissing sound. "But you didn't need our help, mon amie. We watched, and then raced to the beach."

Keelee folded his arms over his chest. "Well, which path do you want to take, Jaden? The one to my right?" Green vines hung from tall trees. Smooth orange and yellow fruit weighed down the branches. "Or the one to my left?" Here the earth was red and sandy. Tall cacti lined a narrow trail.

"Neither. Now I'm hungry. Aren't you?" I eased to the ground, backpack in my lap, proud of my decision.

"Now that you mention it, yes. What do you have a taste for?" He sat, crossed his legs Indian-style on the sand, and adjusted his baseball cap.

"You mean we get a choice?"

"Absolutely. Weejums aim to please." He chuckled.

"Hmmm. Pizza, with cheese and pepperoni."

"Yah. That's sounds great, and Dr. Pepper to drink. Had that before." He pulled his pack off his shoulders and reached inside. Pulling out two cans of soda he said, "Your turn."

I laughed. The packs were wonderful. I could already smell the sauce and melted cheese. Two, eight-inch boxes were inside along with four foil pouches.

"What are those?" Keelee wrinkled his forehead at the smell of fish.

"Dudes!" Slinky looked at us like we were dummies. "Cod and yellow fin tuna."

"Smashing, chums. That's for us." Shakespeare's long pink tongue slid over his mouth.

Keelee smacked his lips opening the pizza box. "Well, like I said, the packs give us what we need. Umm these look yummy."

I took a bite and eyed the two paths. Which one should I choose?

***

What does Jaden do? If she takes the path curving into the jungle, turn to page twenty-three, Chapter Four-A. If she takes the path to the desert, turn to page thirty, Chapter Four-B.

CHAPTER THREE-B

The Red Valley

The trek down the new path led us through a pine forest. Inhaling the smell reminded me of Christmas. Soon I could feel sweat on my forehead. "It's getting warm." I took off my parka and held it up. "Should I put this in my backpack?"

"Yes. Someone else may need it another time." Keelee tucked his jacket into his pack.

"Oh." I grinned and turned to face the trail again. I could see where the forest ended and where there should be a valley. But there wasn't one. Instead, a large patch of red moved up and down a short distance ahead. Black tails disappeared into the woods.

I stopped and put my hands on my hips. "Okay, I have to ask even if you won't have an answer. What's that?" I lifted my chin to the red thing ahead. It looked like a pond, but it was waving too much. And there didn't seem to be a shore, only blue sky at the edges. The shimmering patch of red...turning red-orange...then orange was floating in the air.

Keelee rolled his eyes. "Of course I don't know. If I did this wouldn't be an adventure."

"Smarty pants. Guess you're right, but that makes everything so much harder."

"You aren't whining are you?"

"Never!" I stuck the tip of my tongue out at him. "We better get closer."

Keelee laughed and scooted in front of me, taking the lead. When we were within a hand's reach of the mysterious object, we shouted together, "Butterflies!"

18

"Millions of them." I opened my mouth wide, awed by the sight, then quickly snapped it shut. The flying creatures were surrounding us. I didn't want to swat at the fluttering insects, they were too pretty, but I couldn't move past them.

"Heeelllppp!" Keelee's yellow sneakers lifted two feet into the air. "They've got me."

He rose even higher. The butterflies were carrying him away.

"DT, musketeers, where are you?" I ran then jumped up, trying to grab his shoes. My fingers only touched his heels. "Oh, no!" Keelee drifted above my head.

Leaping into the air, I threw up my arms as far as I could, but couldn't reach him. "Let him go!" I tried to sound real mean.

"Help me," Keelee wailed.

My legs pumped harder. Then four black arrows shot over my head from a nearby tree. The cats hissed and screeched at the butterflies. Their claws snagged Keelee's clothes, and they dangled from him like fishing lures.

"We is wit cha, boss," Blackie said.

The extra weight helped, and Keelee lowered a bit. I sprung into the air again, using all the strength my legs could muster. One of his striped socks was in my grip. I pulled, my heart pounding. At first nothing happened. I tugged harder.

"Hurrah! Gotcha," I bellowed.

Keelee landed on top of me, and we went tumbling down a hill. We landed half way from the bottom with a thump.

I looked for the cats but they were gone again. Then I turned to Keelee. "You okay?"

"Yah." He grabbed my hand, pulling me to my feet. "Let's go. Run!"

When we reached the bottom of the hill we collapsed on a riverbank. The gang of butterflies still swarmed at the top, shimmering like a mango sunset. Resting my head on the cool, green grass, I closed my eyes. I felt the tickle of whiskers on my cheek, and a cold nose nuzzle against my ear—Slinky. As I lifted my head, Blackie pushed my hand with his head, insisting I pet him. DT and Shakespeare stared at the water.

My breathing was ragged as I spoke. "Not a red valley after all."

"Nope." Keelee shook his head and his ears fluttered. "Whities could never come here. They'd melt before they met the butterflies."

I chuckled then rolled onto my tummy and faced the

river. On the other side, shops lined a narrow road. A boy led a pony from Smithy's Livery. Children jumped rope in front of a place called McBride's Dry Goods. The town, with its wooden walkways and dirt street, could have popped out of an old cowboy movie. I hoped Melanie and Snowy were there.

I nudged Keelee. "Looks like we have to cross the river."

"Yep! Beat you to the other side." The Weejum somersaulted to his feet and took a leaping splash into the water. He turned to me as he swam. "Whatcha waiting for, a boat or something? You can swim, right?"

"Yes, but…I'll get all wet and what about the cats?"

"You won't melt." He chuckled. "And I'm sure DT and his gang have a plan."

I grimaced and dove in. Boys! What a pain. They don't understand anything. But soon I smiled. The chilly river felt good on my heated skin. Then a log loaded with cats floated past. I chuckled, watching them wiggle their butts as they shifted their weight to steer.

In no time we were climbing onto a wooden dock. Rowboats with fishing poles poking up from them were tied to thick posts. Funny thing was, my clothes were dry when I got out of the water. Keelee sat on the planking holding his sides laughing.

"You knew." I grabbed his cap and slapped it on his head several times.

"And you don't have much faith. Need to find you some."

"Oh, a wise guy too." I giggled then gulped, looking at the woods that weren't there before. "There's no path leading to the town. What should we do now?" I wrinkled my forehead, disappointed.

"Means we can't go there. Think, Jaden."

Several small, brown critters with flat tails scurried out of the forest. They carried branches in their big teeth. Others were farther down the bank, chomping at small trees. All of the animals were busy working.

I pinched my lips together. "Let's talk to the beavers."

Keelee grinned and nodded.

"Can you help us? We need to find a doll and a kitten." The first beaver didn't answer me. He ran back into the forest.

"Hmmm. Let's try the others building the dam." I wasn't ready to give up and walked to the group. "Can you help us, Mr. Beaver?"

"Not now, lassie. Tis here's a team." The animal swung his furry head at the other beavers. "Gotta a job. Can na stop til we're done."

"But that'll take forever." I frowned.

"Not iffin ya help us."

Photo by Steve Hersey, Washington, DC.
www.booksforamerica.com

"At your service, mes amis." DT and company stretched and kicked up dirt with their back paws.

We made many trips, sprinting to and from the woods with branches. I paused, smiling at my new friends as they whizzed past. The Weejum stopped at my side. "We have a great team, Keelee."

"Think so too." He grinned.

A while later, I wiped my forehead with my shirtsleeve. The work was done. Brown animals stood on the pile of wood in the water with their furry chests puffed out.

I strolled to the dam. "Your house turned out nice, Mr. Beaver. Can you help us now?"

He scratched his fat belly. "Don't know 'bout no doll. Saw a wee lass...brown with mud...ripped dress. Had a cat with her too, busted 'is tail." Then splash, the beavers all dove into the water.

I moaned, "That's awful." But I was afraid I wouldn't get more information so I yelled, "Please, where did you see them?"

Gurgle, splash! A beaver's head poked out from the dam. "Yonder trail into the foothills."

"What trail?" I turned and squinted into the trees. And there it was—a path. "Thank you very much, Mr. Beaver."

Poor Melanie and Snowy. They must have had a rough time. I hoped we'd find them soon and sprinted to catch up with Keelee. As the lane rose upward, the tall pines went away. Low twisted trees took their place. Bees buzzed in patches of sweet-smelling wild flowers and twigs crunched beneath my feet. Finally only a naked, brown mountain stood in front of me.

Keelee shoved his hands into his pockets. "Which way do we turn, my friend?"

I squinted in the bright sun. The paths running along the bottom of the mountain were the same both ways. A wooden post stood near the rocky wall. Rusty nails poked out from it. "There used to be a sign here, but it's gone."

"Maybe not. Look around." Keelee marched in small circles, kicking at the ground. "There's a board sticking up from the dirt on this side." He stooped and brushed off the dust. "It says Very Old."

I found another sign on my side of the post. "This one says Wild."

"Which way Jaden, old or wild?" Keelee grinned.

Oh, geez, another decision. I groaned in my head, not wanting Keelee to think I was whining.

***

If Jaden chooses the Old path, turn to page thirty-seven, Chapter Four-C. If she picks the Wild path, turn to page forty-five, Chapter Four-D.

CHAPTER FOUR-A

The Papaya Jungle

"I've never been in a jungle or a desert before." For a few seconds I stared at both paths. "Oh, look. Pretty flowers are growing in there."

Before I could think again, I saw large bunches of orchids—pink...yellow...purple. As I touched a blossom with my fingertip the decision was made. The desert trail disappeared.

We walked in silence for a few minutes. Plants with large leaves stretched across the path like giant umbrellas. Light sprinkled through the leaves high above, creating shadows. I heard a rustle in the trees ahead and stopped. Then I jumped back, bumping into Keelee. He giggled as a large parrot swooped down and landed on my shoulder.

"Squawk! What do you want here?" the bird asked.

I flinched. The bird's claws tickled and its feathers brushed my cheek. It nuzzled my hair with his beak then flopped into my arms like a baby. I lowered my head slowly not wanting to startle the bird. "We're looking for a doll and a kitten. Have you seen them?"

"Nah, caah, caah." The parrot blinked several times.

"Guess that means no," Keelee said.

The bird hopped off and flew to a nearby papaya tree. "Stay, play." It called, standing on one foot then the other, rustling the leaves in front of it. "Caliopa hide. You find. Can't see me. Caah. Caah."

I giggled. Feathers...bright blue and yellow flashed through the greenery like fireworks. It wasn't possible for the creature to hide anywhere. The parrot was almost as big as Keelee and as colorful.

23

I stepped closer to the limb where the parrot perched. "I'm so sorry we can't stay. We have to find my toys."

"Pretty lady and kitty hiding. Caliopa can't find."

I gulped. "Then you did see them."

"Short time. Ran down path to Rapido's tree."

"Who's that?"

"He good hider. Can't see him in papayas." The bird spread her wings and soared up through the top of the trees. Her shadow lingered for a few seconds then it too was gone.

Caliopa

Photo by Luc Viatour Found at Wikipedia.org
http://www.lucnix.be/main.php

I turned to Keelee and wrinkled my nose. "What do you suppose a Rapido is?"

Keelee scratched his head. "Something that moves very fast?"

We continued along the trail and asked each creature we passed, "Are you Rapido?"

None of the animals answered, neither the orange tree frog, nor the green dragon fly said a word. The monkeys chattered in a language of their own as they swung from the branches. I cupped my hands over my mouth and shouted, "Rapido, where are you?"

Soon I heard a splashing sound, running water. I

24

parted large green leaves with my arms to see farther. "Hmmm, the path ends here."

Water babbled over mossy rocks in a stream about as wide as my driveway at home. I picked up a long branch and poked the water to check the bottom. Some spots were deep.

Several rapidly spinning whirlpools made me dizzy as I watched them. "This doesn't look good. Too far to jump and I'm afraid the swirly parts will pull us under."

"Good point, but swinging is fun. Watch me." Keelee grabbed a thick vine in his fists. He wrapped one leg around it and kicked off with the other. His body flew through the air. He landed with a thump on the other side. "Your turn." He grinned.

It looked too easy. I frowned, then grabbed a vine. I'd climbed ropes in gymnastics class. This shouldn't be any harder than that. I wrapped the vine around my leg and began to swing. My body made large half circles over the creek. Each time my feet dangled over prickly palm shrubs, leaving me nowhere to land.

"What am I going to do, Keelee?"

He sat on the sand and opened his pouch. "There's nothing in here. That means we have to think of something ourselves."

Keelee stood and squinted, looking around. I swung over his head once more while he stared at a rotted tree stump. It might hold his weight. After all, someone two-feet tall weighed next to nothing. He sprinted to the broken tree and pushed. His jaw stiffened as he shoved, but the chuck of wood didn't budge.

"Musketeers, we need you," I shouted.

"Hear ya, darlin'." Slinky eyed my feet and jumped up as I swung past. His claws snagged my shoelaces. With him dangling beneath me, we were easier for Keelee to reach. If only he could get the stump closer to the water.

"I'z da main muscle, pal." Big Blackie nudged Keelee away from the stump. He and Shakespeare began shoving as DT pulled the chunk of wood forward with his claws. Soon the log was in place and Keelee jumped on top.

"Sure hope your idea works. My arms are getting tired." I took a deep breath, curved my back, and swung as hard as I could.

Keelee reached for Slinky. "Now Jaden, let go of the vine!"

I closed my eyes and did. My feet hit the ground first followed by my bottom. I yelped, fearing that I'd squashed

25

Slinky, but he and the other cats had disappeared. I dropped my shoulders onto the sand and rubbed my arms.

"Are you hurt?"

"No, a little sore that's all. Thank you, Keelee." The Weejum cared about me. When I fell off my bike, Marcy laughed. But she was supposed to be my friend?

I stood and could see the path winding into the jungle again. After walking a short while, I heard a chuckle, but couldn't see who made it. I looked harder.

The soft laughter sounded again. "Where are you?" I asked.

"In front of you, amigos."

I put my hand over my eyes, shielding them from the glare of sunlight coming through the trees. Then I saw it. Only a few steps ahead of me, an animal with a flat head, huge eyes, and a silly grin, clung to a branch. It had to be a sloth.

Photo by Stefan Laube (Tauchgurke) Found at
Wikipedia.org

"Oh my!" I stared at the creature. "Have you seen a doll and a kitten?"

The sloth inched closer at the speed of a snail. "Si señor, senorita."

"You can't be Rapido. Can you?" Keelee asked.

"Si. Caliopa, my beautiful amiga, she eez funny, no?"

"Yes, I guess she is, but have you seen my toys?"

"They run to the reever. Faster than I, amigos."

"But we just crossed the river." Keelee placed his fist on his hip and his jaw tightened.

The sloth shook his head. "No, no. That jus a leetle finger. Ju follow the trail." He pointed his long-clawed paw in the direction we were headed.

"Thank you Rapido." I smiled and grabbed Keelee's hand. "Let's go."

I skipped and Keelee bobbed along with me. Four cats appeared and sniffed the ground as they zigzagged ahead. Patches of dry grass began to take away the path. The landscape started to change, and I inhaled new fragrances. Junipers, magnolias and cypress trees replaced the vines and the papayas. As I paused to check the area, gray squirrels scampered across the sandy trail and brown toads croaked in a patch of tall grass. The cats made a wild dash after them.

"This place looks familiar, but how could that be?" I asked.

"Maybe we're getting close to where Melanie and Snowy were lost?"

My heart skipped a beat. "You think so?"

"Sure."

"Then come on, let's run."

Sand flew through the air behind us as we sprinted. The sound of splashes echoed in my ears. I ran up a small hill. A slow moving river shaded by high tree branches lay at the bottom. A nutria popped its head out of the water and ambled onto the bank. It shook the water from its beaver-like body, spraying the brush. Then the rodent stood on its hind legs and stared at me with round black eyes. His whiskers twitched as I came closer.

"My friends and I ride bikes in a park like this, but there's no path to follow anymore." My eyebrows pinched together as I looked to the right, and then to the left. "What do we do now?"

Keelee sat on the ground, bent his knee, and rested his elbow on top of it. "What did you do the last time you were here?"

I sat next to him and closed my eyes. Minutes passed. "I can't remember. Maybe if we walked more it'll come back."

"Which way?"

Photo by Petar Milosecevic Found at Wikipedia.org

"Oh geez, not that again." My shoulders slumped, but then I gasped. A young girl wearing a purple ball cap walked on the other side of the river. Her clothes were funny. A small person dressed in the same outfit held her hand. My eyes widened. The child wasn't a baby—he was Keelee. "Oh my gosh!"

"Not a problem." The Weejum rose to his feet. "But you have to pick which side of the water you want to be on."

"What happens if we cross over to them?"

"They disappear. There can't be two of us at the same time. One path will be gone."

"But what if Melanie and Snowy are on this side?" I rubbed my cheek in frustration. Tears were starting to fill my eyes. I took a deep breath. No way was I going to cry.

Keelee reached his arm around my waist. "Sometimes you have to trust your heart. Like you did when you chose to come with us." His eyes sparkled and he was wearing a soft smile.

I nodded, knowing he was right, but that didn't make deciding easy. The cats wandered back and sat with their tails wrapped around their front paws. They looked at me with sad eyes and meowed. Choking back the lump in my throat, I stood and petted all of their heads.

I reached for my backpack, but it was no longer there. Keelee's bag was gone too, and then so were the cats. "No more help, huh?"

"Nope. And only one path to follow. Here or over there." Keelee pointed his chin at the girl and small boy across the river.

***

Continue on page fifty-one, Chapter Five.

CHAPTER FOUR-B

The Orange Desert

I walked along the dusty path. Fat cacti lined the trail two or three thick, and I couldn't see past them. My yellow sneakers were covered in red sand. I tasted the bitter desert soil on my lips. Then the rows of prickly plants ended, letting me see the land around us.

I stopped to take it all in. "It's so beautiful here. I've never seen anything like this before." Orange and red rocks grew out of the flat ground. Some of them sat on top of each other looking like they might fall at any minute. Between the clumps of giant stones, short trees, tall grass, and wild flowers grew. Farther away, high mountains, some with white pointed tops, made a zigzagged line across the blue sky.

Keelee looked at the highest mountain peek. "Some children called this place Colorado. Things have come up missing from a city nearby. But in my world you can never be sure exactly where you are."

I took the lead. After walking a short while, there were no edges on the ground to show where to step. The path was gone. I frowned and looked back. Nothing was there but air.

"Now what, Keelee?"

"Shush." He lifted the flap on his ear. "Hear that?"

I stood perfectly still. "It sounds like someone is crying."

He jumped over low boulders, tiptoed around a fat cactus, and then listened again. "It's coming from behind those rocks."

I sprinted to where Keelee pointed, and he followed. A small prairie dog sat on a dry piece of wood. It held its face in its paws and its shoulders were shaking.

30

"Little prairie dog, why are you crying?" I took slow steps toward the animal, not wanting to frighten it, and not knowing if it could understand me.

The animal sniffled and swiped at its nose with its paw. "I'm lost. I'll miss the big party and everything." The prairie dog lowered its eyes and started to sob all over again.

I squatted beside it. "What's your name? Maybe we can help you find your home. Have you any idea where that is?"

Photo by Steve Polkinghorne, Devon, UK

"My name is Misha, and my town is near the hogback rocks. They're supposed to look like camels so people say, but I don't know what a camel is. Do you?"

"Yes." The prairie dog's dark brown eyes seemed to brighten with hope. I looked around, but nothing looked like a camel. Red, blue, and orange rocks, all pointy, filled the area. Large clumps of stones blocked my view of what lie ahead. I peeked into my backpack. Darn, it was empty.

I turned to Keelee. "Any ideas?"

"Maybe if we were higher, we could see farther."

"Perfect." I popped up with a big smile. "I can use that pile of rocks over there."

"Be careful, Jaden. Some of those boulders could be

loose."

"I will." I scampered over to the hill and began to climb.

I wanted to ask Misha about Melanie and Snowy, but that would have to wait. The pup looked so sad. There had to a way for Keelee and I to help the small creature. Then I slipped on a loose stone as Keelee had warned. My feet slid out from under me and my arms flew into the air. I reached for a bush to keep from sliding all the way down, but the branch was slippery and slid through my fingers.

"We's wit cha, doll." Blackie threw his big body across my path.

"Blimey!" Shakespeare pounced on Blackie's back adding his weight to the pile.

I stopped sliding, but my knees scraped the rocks, making them sting. DT and Slinky licked them through my torn pants as if they wanted to make the hurt go away. That was so sweet of them.

After brushing the dust from my green pants, I scratched my pals behind their ears. "Thank you, guys. You're really good friends." They all purred softly, then dashed off.

"Are you okay?" Keelee hollered.

"Yes." Feeling my face get warm, I tried to hide my embarrassment. I looked down and he wasn't laughing like Marcy had been. Maybe she wasn't my friend after all.

"Can you see rocks that look like camels?"

I blocked the sun from my eyes with my hand. "No, not yet. I'll go higher."

I grabbed the rock ledge and pulled myself up. This time I climbed slower, pushing down on the stones with my hands to be sure they weren't loose. When I was higher, I stood as tall as I could and looked around.

"I see two humps, the camel rocks. Hurray!" I wanted to jump up and down, but didn't dare loosen anything. From below I could hear Keelee and the prairie dog clapping. I inched my way back down the pile of rocks.

"Your home is far away, too long a walk for a prairie dog as little as you. How did you get here, anyway?"

Misha lowered her head. "Chasing a beetle. Mamma said not to do that, but it was so cute. I wanted the funny bug to play with me. Then I got lost."

Camel Back Rocks

Photo by David Shankbone Found at Wikipedia.org

"Guess mommies and daddies are right, but I don't always do what they say either." Like I shouldn't take Grandma's toys outside, but I didn't say that. "Did you see a doll and kitten?" I crossed my fingers behind my back.

"No."

My heart sank to my toes.

Keelee reached over his shoulder for the strap on his bag. "Before we go anywhere, my throat is dry and my stomach's grumbling." He opened his backpack. "I have two bottles of something called Gatorade." One of his eyebrows lifted. "What's that? Made from Alligators?"

Even though I was worried about Melanie, and not having any new clues, I couldn't help but giggle. "No, yuk. It's like the sodas, but without the bubbles. You drink it when you're thirsty and need energy. What else do you have?"

"A fist full of daisies." He pulled them out.

"That's for me." Misha held out her tiny paws. "I get both food and water from them." She stuffed a bunch of flowers into her mouth and began chewing.

I looked in my pack and smelled peanuts and grapes. My mouth watered. "Peanut butter and jelly sandwiches and Black-eyed Susans." I grinned. "I guess these flowers are for you too, Misha."

I settled on a log and Keelee joined me. Maybe I made a wrong decision choosing this path. So far we had no clues about Melanie and Snowy, but I'm glad we'd come this way for Misha's sake.

I nudged Keelee. "We don't have anything for the

cats."

"They'll be okay. Think they'd scare the fur off the prairie dog so they're hiding."

I nodded. We ate and drank before starting our journey. Misha rode in Keelee's backpack. After a while, I climbed another pile of rocks to be sure we were still going the right way. From the top, I could see a very large circle of sand dotted with round hills of dirt. Next to the hills, hundreds of prairie dogs stood up on their back legs.

"We'll be at your town soon," I said.

"Yippee," Misha chirped.

Keelee and I jogged toward the colony. When we were close, Keelee lowered his backpack and let Misha run on ahead. A loud ruckus filled the air. Prairie dogs talked, making barking and chirping sounds.

"Come meet my family," Misha hollered above the noise.

I crept forward not knowing what to expect. I'd seen a few of the creatures in the zoo back home, but never saw so many of them at one time. A chubby brown prairie dog, larger than most, with a deep voice spoke first.

"Name's General Malcum Brown. Thank you for returning our daughter. How can we repay you?"

Many prairie dogs stood at attention on top of hills, little warriors guarding their homes. Misha wrapped her front paw around the middle of another prairie dog a bit smaller than the General. This one stooped and hugged the little one tightly.

I smiled. "We could use your help finding a lost doll and a kitten. Have you seen them?"

The General scratched his head. "Can't say that I have."

Three small prairie dogs scampered forward. "Sir, we saw a lady and a white cat at the river."

I frowned. "Oh no. I saw another river when I was on top of the rocks, but it's so far away, Keelee. We'll never get there before morning."

"We know a short cut." One of the pups chattered.

"The back door to our house ends up there." The second one chirped.

"Come on follow us." Misha and the third youngster barked before dropping into a burrow.

Keelee sprinted for the hole as if nothing was wrong. "Wait. We can't fit in there. We're too big," I said.

"Sure we can. Watch." Keelee stepped to the hole and dropped from sight. "Come on, Jaden. Have some faith."

I stood staring at the opening. This can't be possible. The hole was only as big as my toes. As I slid one foot forward, a whooshing sound echoed in my ears. Then I was sliding under the ground. The tunnel was smooth and smelled like cut grass. At the bottom, I stood, but I couldn't see a thing in the dark. Keelee reached for my hand and pulled me along at a run.

My heart beat so hard I thought it would pop out of my chest. "Slow down, Keelee. What if we hit a wall or fall into a hole?" I didn't ask him about the other nasty critters that live in the ground like fat spiders.

"You worry too much."

I guess I did, and decided to try having faith for a change. Minutes passed as we ran. The tapping of many feet and paws on the hard ground were the only sounds for a while. Then I heard splashes as if water were hitting a bank somewhere.

"We're almost there." Misha tugged my pant leg, smiling.

Then in an instant the prairie dogs were gone. Light sprinkled through an opening around a curve in the passage, and Keelee sped on ahead.

"I see a river. Fish are jumping up from the water and everything," he called back.

Stepping from the hole, I squinted in the bright sunshine. I blinked as I gazed at the change in the scenery. Cypress trees replaced the cacti. The dry desert sand was gone. I pressed the toe of my yellow sneaker into black damp earth. Birds chirped, and a red squirrel darted into a clump of bushes.

Nearby, a brown beaver-like face poked its head through the ripples in the gently flowing water. The nutria swam to shore (picture is on page twenty-eight). I stared at the creature in disbelief. He seemed to have winked at me.

"I think I know this place." I strolled a short distance along the river, then turned to the Weejum. "I ride my bike in this park with my friends, but we're in your world not mine."

"Maybe not. Look across the water at the path on that side."

I saw a girl wearing colorful clothes. She held the hand of a small person wearing a matching outfit.

My eyes darted to Keelee and I stammered. "That's us...isn't it...but we're here too?"

"Looks like you have to choose which side of the river we need to be on. I think we're close to Melanie and Snowy now."

"Me too. Shush. I can hear my doll calling me."

"Come find me Jaden. I can't get out by myself." A kitten meowed in the background.

I gazed at the couple on the other side of the river and rubbed my eyes with my fists. Tears were starting to wet my eyes, but I was determined not to cry. "I'm afraid I'll pick wrong, and then I'll never find them."

Keelee placed his hand on my shoulder and patted it gently. "Did you make bad decisions so far?"

"I don't think so. We've gotten this close to my toys."

"Then believe you'll find a way to make things right when they're wrong."

I smiled. "You're a great friend, Keelee."

"Thanks."

I turned from the Weejum and studied both sides of the river.

***

Continue on page fifty-one, Chapter Five.

CHAPTER FOUR-C

Ancient Cavern

I placed one hand on each side of my face. Everywhere on the trail, white flowers filled the trees. I recognized the dogwoods with their pink edged petals, but had never seen the others. "It's springtime here, but it's summer at home." My voice was a small whisper full of surprise.

"That happens sometimes. Makes things more interesting." Keelee picked a blossom and held it out to me.

I smiled, tucking it behind my ear.

DT popped out from under a bush and waved his feathered cap as he bowed. "We're back, mes amis."

The four cats and I followed the Weejum along the pebble-strewn passage. In a while, heavy dark clouds began to block out the sun. The wind howled. Sand stung my cheeks. I heard a loud rumble, then lightening blazed like white fire across the sky.

"We'd better look for shelter," Keelee said. "Nasty weather's coming." He left the path and began walking close to the mountain, spreading apart the branches of bushes. The cats darted in and out with their noses pressed to the ground.

"What are you looking for? We can't hide under a tree in a thunderstorm. Lightening might hit us."

"There are caves in these hills. I reckon to find us one." Keelee dropped to his knees and crawled beneath a juniper. "Just the thing. Come on, Jaden."

I got on my hands and knees and squeezed into the opening he made. Brambles poked my head and pickers stuck to my clothes. "Are you sure this will work?"

"Absolutely—unless you're afraid of bats."

37

"Yikes!" I yelped. "I never saw one for real, only in picture books, but they looked scary."

"Bats are cool dudes!" Slinky sniffed, making his whiskers twitch.

Keelee glanced over his shoulder and grinned. "We look pretty scary to them too. Don't think they'll bother us." He turned and kept crawling forward. "Found an opening." The Weejum disappeared through a gap in the gray stone.

Peeking in, I whispered, "Wow."

I saw a room with rough, stone walls. The high, curved ceiling had holes that let in light, but not much. At least I was glad there were no bats. I crawled inside. The dirt floor was covered with branches as if animals had built nests inside. I wondered what kind of creatures they were. I shuddered, hoping bears or bobcats weren't some of them. The cats sniffed around and chased bugs.

Keelee sat against the wall and opened his pack. "Not much in here, only two bottles of orange juice. "What's in your bag?"

I sat next to him and unzipped my sack. "Four packages of peanut butter crackers."

"Yummy," he said.

As we ate, thunder rumbled outside, and I heard the loud sound of pounding rain. Water poured through a hole in the ceiling. I held my breath as I watched the puddle beneath it get bigger. The cats lapped the water not seeming to notice.

"The cave won't flood, will it?" My voice was small and filled with dread.

"Never has before."

"You mean you've been here?"

"Not in this cave exactly, but the backpacks take care of us, remember. You have to trust them, and yourself too." He winked and bit into a cracker with a crunch.

I took the bottle of juice and began to explore the open space, then heard a rattling sound. The cats raced to the doorway. Their backs curved up making them look bigger.

"Ged outa here!" Blackie snarled.

The other cats hissed, their white fangs glistened in the dim light. A brown snake with diamonds on its back hissed too. It shoved its red forked tongue in and out of its mouth. The rattle on its tail moved faster.

I was so afraid the snake would bite the cats a sour taste filled my mouth.

Ancient Cavern

Photo by Dave Bunnell, Underearth Images,
www.underearth.us

"Do something Jaden," Keelee whispered.

This time I didn't worry about the decision being up to me. I stooped, grabbed a rock, and pitched it at the snake as hard as I could. I missed! I found another one. Missed again. How can I be so bad at this? I felt like screaming. The snake hissed louder. DT and his gang shimmied back, but the rattler could still reach them.

Biting my bottom lip, I threw another rock. This time the stone landed close. The snake made a circle with its body. My heart pounded. It hissed one more time, showing its nasty fangs, then slithered back outside.

"Great work, Jaden." Keelee raised his palm for a high five.

"Bloody good show!"

"Cool, Dude!"

"Tanks, doll face!"

DT circled my feet and rubbed my legs with his face. "Merci, mon amie. That means thanks."

"You're welcome." I smiled, my chest filled with warm fuzzies.

I sat against the cave wall and took a long drink of juice. Looking around, I saw that smooth rock made shelves around the walls. Here and there a black cubbyhole, that might lead somewhere, dotted the stone. In one corner, rain poured in from the ceiling making a gentle waterfall. As the droplets splashed into a pool, they glittered as if this were a fairyland. Then I noticed an opening behind the wet stream and walked to it.

"Oh, no! A skunk." I held my nose as I stumbled backward, preparing for the awful stink. The black animal with two white stripes on its back strolled into the cavern. The racket I made didn't stop the critter. As it took a drink from the pool, it lifted its tail.

I huddled near Keelee. "We're in big trouble now." My hands flew to my face, and I lowered my head.

Swish...whoosh...the air filled with white vapor. I coughed, needing to breathe, but the first whiff startled me. My jaw dropped as I smelled the air again.

"I can't believe it. I smell coconuts."

"Vat else dahlink?" The skunk opened and closed its eyes several times as if it were batting its lashes. "Vat arr you doing here?"

"Umm...uh," I stammered.

Keelee stood and strutted to where we were standing. He crouched and talked to the skunk. "My friend is trying to say we're looking for a doll and a kitten. Have you seen them?"

The skunk waived her tail like a ribbon in a gentle

breeze. "Not I, but perhaps one of my sweet ones have. Lilac, Cinnamon, Jasmine come to mamma plis."

Three more skunks scurried into the room. They were much smaller and their stripes were all different. The last one was completely black with the fluffiest white tail I'd ever seen.

"Show our guests your talents, dahlinks."

All three animals lifted their bottoms and tails. One at a time, they sprayed smells that matched their names. Lilacs like the shampoo my mommy buys me, cinnamon sticky buns, and the sweet flowers that cover the fence in my backyard at home.

Jasmine and Cinnamon

Photo by http://www.birdphotos.com Found at Wikipedia.org

"That's so wonderful." I clapped my hands, then looked at the mama and asked, "Is your name Coconut?"

"Yes." The skunk slinked forward swaying her hips. "Vant I show you how eez done?"

I gulped and could feel my face turning red. "I don't think so, but thank you. We're on a mission."

Keelee began chuckling. I rolled my eyes at him, then turned to the critters. "Have any of you seen a doll and a kitten?"

"Yah, zee river. Come." Lilac went racing to the opening in the cave wall and disappeared. The other two animals were on her tail.

Keelee grabbed my hand and soon we were stumbling in total darkness. He stopped quickly when all the light was gone. I bumped into him almost falling over.

"Found a flashlight in my pack." He clicked it on. "Check yours."

Sure enough, I had one too. I aimed the light all around us. Straight ahead was an opening to a small tunnel. I peeked inside. The floor sloped downward. "We might be able to fit if we crawled on our stomachs."

Keelee went in first. "Jeepers. At least there aren't any bats in here."

"That makes me feel better." I clicked my tongue against the roof of my mouth. "Let's go before we lose the little skunks."

Smooth rock surrounded me like a cocoon wrapped around a caterpillar. I wiggled my hips, copying the movement of the snake, and shoved against the rock floor with my toes. My elbows were getting sore; the walls smelled bad. I shivered in the cold air that seemed to close in on me and didn't know how much longer I could stand it. The cocoon didn't feel so cozy any more.

Finally, the ceiling was high enough for Keelee to stand up. After a short distance, I was able to do the same. I breathed a sigh of relief as I got to my feet, but the happiness didn't last. My body began to teeter. Green slime shimmered beneath my yellow sneakers, wet and slippery. The slant of the floor got bigger and my feet flew into the air.

"Keelee, I hope you're behind me."

"Yep. Wow this is awesome." He whooped and hollered. Boys!

The slide in the rock wound around in tight circles. I seemed to be on a sled, but my bottom was the thing that slid. The ride lasted so long I felt dizzy. Then I sailed through the air and hit the water with a loud splash. Before I could tell what was happening and be afraid, the cool liquid covered me, and my feet hit a sandy bottom. I kicked off and splashed through the surface faster than a shooting star. Keelee's head popped up seconds later. He coughed and laughed at the same time.

I looked around as I swam to the shore. Cypress trees stood where the flowered ones used to be. I grabbed the gnarled roots, pulling my body onto dry ground. Keelee struggled in the mud. His shoes made slurpy sounds, so I reached out and pulled him along side me.

He shook the water from his floppy ears like a puppy. "That was a heck of ride."

"I hate to admit it, but it was fun." I grinned sheepishly. "But I'm glad it's over."

We took off our backpacks and set them in the sun. In seconds, four cats pounced on them. They lounged in a big pile. Some were belly up, but all were purring.

Leaning back on my elbows, I watched my clothes dry. Wet dark patches became light as the water lifted in a mist and floated away. Amazing. As I gazed at the river, a gray squirrel scampered up a tree. White swans and ducks floated by. A brown, furry head poked out of the water. His fat beaver-like body waddled onto the sand. He sat up on his hind legs and stared at me.

I whispered, "It's a nutria (picture is on page twenty-eight). This looks like the park where I ride my bike with my friends. But it can't be, we're in your world."

Keelee chuckled. "Maybe, maybe not. Look across the river."

I shaded my eyes to block the bright sun. A girl dressed in funny clothes held the hand of a small child. My glance drifted to my own outfit. They were the same. It can't be. The pair strolled closer to where Keelee and I sat, and I could see that the shorter person wasn't a baby at all, but a Weejum.

"Oh my gosh, that's us!"

"Not really, but you have to choose which side of the river you want to be on. Here or over there." He stretched his arm toward the water.

My throat became dry. "This is so hard. What will happen to them if we swim across?"

"It'll be like they never were. Like the paths you didn't choose, they melt away."

I rubbed my fist against my forehead and closed my eyes to push back my tears. No way was I going to cry! "We're close to Melanie and Snowy. I can feel it. What if I choose the wrong side?"

"Then you'll find a way to make it right."

43

I smiled, feeling better, but that didn't make deciding easier. "Thanks for being my friend, Keelee."

Our backpacks began to shimmer. The cats stood, and DT bowed one last time before they all disappeared.

***

Continue on page fifty-one, Chapter Five.

CHAPTER FOUR-D

Wild Horse Marsh

I felt a cool breeze on my neck and smelled salty air and fish. Before, the ground had been dark and rocky. Now my feet crunched light sand. We had been in the foothills heading south, but the mountain was no longer there. A live oak forest with scrub palms and holly bushes edged the path and blocked my view. I knew the green, grassy valley we'd seen before might not be there anymore, but what was?

"Where do you think we are, Keelee?"

"Let's stop and listen."

I stood still. "I hear squawking—maybe seagulls?"

"Could be waves hitting a beach too." He hopped ahead of me and began to march. His knees lifted as he marched, and he whistled Yankee Doodle. I giggled, following him. Excitement filled my chest. I loved the beach and could stay and play in the water forever. Soon the tall trees disappeared and in their place were swaying grasses. Dark mud and patches of tall blades stretched between where we stood and a ribbon of white silvery sand.

Keelee stopped at the edge of the marsh. "Must be low tide or this grassy plain would be covered in water."

"Should we try to get to the beach? I don't see a path anymore." I stuck the toe of one sneaker into the mud ahead and pressed down. My shoe made a slurping, squishy sound as I pulled it out. "I don't think we can walk on this ground without getting stuck. Maybe that means we shouldn't go to the shore, but then where should we go?"

"That's a whole bunch of questions I don't have answers for as usual." Keelee pressed his lips together and his brow pinched as he looked around. He ambled to an old log, sat, and unzipped his backpack. "Just what we need." His eyes brows lifted as he looked inside.

I sat next to him and pulled shiny red boots from my bag. After I tugged them on, I shoved my sneakers into the sack.

"Wait, we may need something else." I sprinted to the woods and found two thick sticks to use as walking poles. "Here, Keelee. In case we get stuck." I knew he wouldn't care if he fell in the icky stuff, but I would.

Keelee grabbed his stick near the top and swung his body over a bunch of marsh grass. "Whoopee. Thanks."

I rolled my eyes. Sea oats swayed in the wind on white dunes not far away. As we came closer, I heard a whinny and thrashing sounds. Globs of wet mud shot into the air.

I parted the green blades with my pole. "It's a little horse. He's stuck in a hole in the mud. We have to help him."

"Tide is coming in. We'd better hurry, Jaden. We have to get to the dunes."

"Why? We can all swim. Can't we?"

"Not with alligators," he said.

"Oh, yikes, and there's nothing more to help us in my pack."

"Think of something, Jaden. You have to." Keelee squealed, watching the animal struggle.

"I have an idea. I'll make him a walkway. Try to keep him calm."

As Keelee spoke softly to the colt, I sloshed back to the woods.

Blackie strutted along side me. "Whatcha need, boss?"

"Branches and lots of them."

"Ya got it."

The cats fetched as many pieces of wood as I could carry, and we made it back to where Keelee and the horse were standing. My arms ached from the heaviness of the wood, but I held on. The Weejum spread them out like a floor in front of the colt.

DT danced and waved his hat, urging the horse forward. I stood near the animal's rump and pushed. Keelee splashed his way to the colt's front and pulled.

The horse whinnied again. His nostrils got big, and I

could tell by his eyes that he was afraid. I tried lifting his back leg, but I couldn't get it onto the branches.

"What are we going to do, Keelee? I'm out of ideas," I wailed.

Then I heard a thunder of hoofs behind us. We both turned to the sound. A much louder whinny, more of war cry, rumbled in my ears. As I stumbled away from the charging horse, I grabbed Keelee's suspenders and pulled him with me.

I watched a large brown mare walk to the colt's rear. The horse lowered her head and butted his behind with a firm snort. The young animal made a shrill, unhappy sound, but quickly bolted onto the branches Keelee had set in front of him. Together, the large and the small horses splashed their way to the dunes.

The two animals stood in the sea oats, manes moving in the wind like flags, waiting for us. Keelee reached for my hand, and we trudged our way to the safety of the high sand.

I breathed a sigh of relief then quickly held my ears. In seconds the sky became dark. Boom, boom, boom, the sound of cannons came from the sea. I dropped to my stomach pulling Keelee with me as orange flames shot across the sky.

My heart pounded as I lifted my head and stared at the ocean. The water was empty. Even the sea birds had flown away. What made those horrible explosions? Next I heard angry shouts and the banging of metal against metal. I should have seen hundreds of people from the sound of the noise, but no one was there.

I covered my head with my arms. "What's going on?"

The voice I heard wasn't Keelee's. It was male, but much deeper than the Weejum's. His tone was gentle, yet he got my full attention. "The ghosts of long ago. Some call them Haints. Don't worry, you won't be hurt by the pirates or the Indians who once lived here."

I looked up at the huge, brown stallion with awe. My words squeaked from my throat. "Why are they doing that?"

"To keep away people that would spoil their land. Only those who respect the beauty of the wilderness are allowed to stay."

Then the stallion scraped the sand with his hoofs and raised his front legs into the air. His nostrils got big, and he gave out a sound I'd never heard before. I trembled and clutched Keelee's hand.

Edited Photo Courtesy of the Galt Museum Archives

"You are safe, little ones. I am Dondero. What has brought you to my shores?"

I stood, lifting my body on wobbly legs. "We're looking for a doll and a kitten."

"Why have you chosen my island for your search?"

I looked at Keelee for help with that question. He stood tall, shoulders back and said, "My people help find lost toys that are loved by the children who own them. The paths we followed led us here."

"Loved? Why?" The stallion stared at me.

"Melanie's so pretty with shiny curls the color of maple syrup, and sky blue eyes. Her soft pink, flowered dress is covered by a lacy, white pinafore."

"And the animal with her?"

"Snowy is cute. Melanie pushes him in a white carriage and he looks up at her like she's his mom. The kitten wears a wreath of tiny, pink roses tied in ribbons around his neck."

The large horse huffed. "They may not be as you remembered, will that matter?"

My heart dropped to my toes, and I bit my thumbnail. I wondered how bad they looked now. "No." I shook my head, but I wasn't sure. Finding them was important. They were a gift from my grandmother, and she'd taken good care of Melanie and Snowy for many years so she could pass them on to me.

"If that's the case, I saw them near the flowing fresh water."

My throat got dry as I spoke. The huge animal made me afraid, but I knew that's not what he wanted. "How can we get there?"

"Climb onto my back and I will take you."

"Thank you so much." I smiled bigger than I had during the whole adventure.

Dondero lowered his front knees to the sand and Keelee and I climbed onto his back. I clutched the horse's scratchy mane while the Weejum wrapped his arms around my waist. The wind roared in my ears as the stallion galloped away from the dunes. I closed my eyes. The air stung my cheeks as we seemed to soar across the ground.

When the horse stopped. I heard birds chirping in cypress trees. A shaded river flowed lazily in front of me. The water lapped at the bank in tiny splashes.

Keelee and I slid from the horse's back. "Thank you, Dondero."

He nodded at both of us. "Good luck with your quest."

Tiny stars twinkled where the stallion stood, then he was gone. In his place, two squirrels scampered across the ground and chased each other up a tree. Swans and ducks swam on the river. A brown critter lifted his beaver-like head from the water and ambled to the shore. The animal stood on his hind legs, front paws pressed against his chest, and seemed to smile at me (picture is on page twenty-eight).

I gasped as I took everything in. "That's a nutria. I've been here before, lots of times with my friends. I'm sure of it."

"Look across the river, Jaden." Keelee leaned against a tree and folded his arms on his chest.

A girl, the same size as me, tossed a pebble into the water. I heard a giggle and the shorter person at her side made a stone skip across the river. Then two purple caps waved in the air, and the girl and her small friend smiled at us.

"They're you and I, Keelee. How can that be?"

"We're close to Melanie and Snowy. It's time for your final choice."

"What do you mean?" As I asked the question I felt my backpack disappear. I glanced at the Weejum. His sack was gone too. "And the cats?"

"Back at the adoption center. You have to decide which side of the river you want to be on." Keelee's voice was as soft as the wings of a butterfly.

I looked at both shores and rubbed my cheek. "How can I know for sure which side is right to find my toys?"

"You can't. Now you have to trust your heart."

"But what if I'm wrong? Will Melanie and Snowy be lost forever?"

"Aw Jaden, don't look so sad. Have you made bad decisions so far?"

Biting back tears, I sank to the ground. No way was I going to cry! "The choices I've made got us this close, so maybe I did okay, but this is hard."

The Weejum stood at my side and wrapped his arm around my shoulder. "Yes it is, but you can do it."

"Thanks for having faith in me, Keelee." I hugged him. My eyes drifted to the paths on both banks to choose.

***

Continue on the next page.

CHAPTER FIVE

The Other Side

I sat on the bank of the river with my arms wrapped around my knees, looking at both sides of the water. The trees, grasses and shrubs, even the mocking birds fluttering in the leaves, seemed the same. Where Keelee and I sat, the river was narrow. I didn't know how deep it was, but there didn't seem to be anything scary about it. Maybe the water was shallow enough for us to walk across?

"Well, what's your decision, Jaden?"

"Let's cross. To stay on this side seems too easy."

"Okay, but we might get wet. Our backpacks disappeared, so there's no Weejum magic to keep us dry."

"So what. I've been wet before, and I know you don't mind being drippy at all."

Keelee chuckled, big dimples formed in his cheeks. "Nope."

I stepped into the river. "Brr, the water's cold."

I lifted my sneaker and sure enough it was soaked. Soon the water was up to my knees. As I moved forward, my feet slid sideways on moss-covered rocks. I waved my arms in the air for a few seconds trying not to fall, but couldn't help it. My behind went splashing into the river. I coughed, wiping the water from my eyes. Then my heart began to beat faster. I couldn't see the Weejum.

"Keelee?" He was so small that the water must be over his head. "Where are you?"

I heard the sound of bubbles, then a whoosh as Keelee's head popped out of the water. He swam to the shore and flopped onto the bank. I leaned forward and dog-paddled, not letting my feet touch the slimy river bottom. With mud dripping from my hair, I crawled next to him.

I winced, looking at my clothes then at his. "Pee ewe. We're yucky and smell like fish."

"Can't be helped. Let's go find Melanie and Snowy. They won't care what we look like," Keelee said with a grin. He wiped his hands on his pants and began to walk along the river.

I slid my palms against my clothes, trying to get rid of as much water as I could. My feet sloshed in my shoes as I hurried to catch up to Keelee. As we walked, I looked across the water. The other shore didn't disappear as paths not chosen had before. What was happening? Had I made the wrong decision?

***

A few minutes passed, then I saw a large fish jump from the water. Rainbow colored scales glistened in the sunlight as its tail splashed the surface. "Did you see that?"

Keelee's eyes were glued to the other side as if he were waiting for the fish to jump again. "Yes, near that floating log."

I wrinkled my nose. "No, that's not the spot. The fish jumped near this shore."

"Must have been two of them." He shrugged his shoulders.

"Maybe?"

I felt a tickle in my tummy, the one I had when things weren't as they should be. Tree branches reached across the water meeting in the middle. Long shadows stretched into the river from both banks. Something about that struck me as strange, but I didn't know what. Then I saw a sandy hill I'd seen before.

I moaned. "Oh, no. I remember something. See that hill over there? I rode my bicycle and fell. My tires caught on a tree root and I went flying."

"Why's that important?"

"Melanie and Snowy were wrapped in blanket in my bike's basket. I forgot about them because I hurt my knee and elbows." I winced, knowing I also forgot because Marcy was laughing at me.

Keelee's eyes brightened. "Do you think they could

have fallen out and that's how they got lost?"

"Sure. That's why Melanie said she was cold, and that sand and dirt were everywhere. We have to swim across. The hill is on the other side."

I dashed to the water, but the Weejum grabbed my orange suspenders before I got very far. "Look at the river, Jaden. Don't you see anything odd?"

"I thought I did but..."

Keelee picked up a pebble and made the stone skip across the water. The little rock stopped in mid-air half way across and plunked into the river. Another stone flew towards it at the same time and bumped into the rock Keelee had thrown.

"Oh...and the shadows of the trees. That's why they come from both sides. Like the two fish, we're seeing things in a mirror." I covered my mouth with my hand. "There's really only one side."

"Yes," Keelee chuckled. "Guess you couldn't make a wrong choice after all. Let's find the hill. We can't see it from where we're standing."

I smiled, stooped, and hugged him. He shuffled his feet and squirmed a little, but was smiling too. I glanced at the hill across the water, then at the same spot on the side we were on. As I ran, I brushed tall grass out of my way and jumped over fallen branches. Soon, white sand covered my sneakers and the ground started to slope upward. I hiked up the hill, my heart pounding. Melanie and Snowy were here. I knew it.

"Here's the tree root that made me fall off my bike, Keelee. And down there, see the broken bushes. That's where I landed."

I spread the twigs and brush along the way, hoping to find my toys. Keelee helped. Melanie and Snowy didn't seem to be here. I dropped to the ground. My shoulders sagged with disappointment.

"Why don't you call Melanie, Jaden?"

"Good idea, Keelee." I cupped my hands around my mouth and shouted, "Melanie where are you. Can you hear me?"

A small voice came from a pile of logs at the river's edge. "Jaden, we're here. Please come get us."

I jumped up, holding my breath, and dashed to the piled of wood. Keelee was beside me, helping to lift the logs.

We grunted, struggling to move the last chunk. A piece of glass glittered in the damp soil where the log had been. I began to cry as I lifted the broken kitten tail.

"Oh, poor Snowy." I pushed back my tears and pleaded, "Melanie, I can't find you. Call me again."

"I'm under the mud. Dig, Jaden."

I sank to my knees and scooped away handfuls of soil. The doll had to be here. "Help me, Keelee."

Black mud flew in the air. Our hands were a blur as we made a wide hole. The edge of a cloth appeared. Melanie's dress and pinafore were no longer pink and white. As I scraped away more dirt, a tiny arm poked out.

"Melanie, I found you," I screamed lifting the doll. "Where's your kitten?"

"He's under me."

"Oh my gosh!" I handed the doll to Keelee, then dug deeper.

Pointed ears stuck up from the hole. I pried the toy animal loose. He looked dreadful. His flowered wreath was covered in burs, and his once shiny white coat was brown. Melanie's pretty hair was matted and covered in mud. Her beautiful dress was torn, and scratches covered her face and arms.

"I'm so sorry, Melanie. You must have fallen out of my basket when I fell. I shouldn't have taken you with me to begin with."

"I know we both look awful, but do you still love us, Jaden?"

"Of course I do." I scooped the two toys into my arms and kissed both of them. "I can give you a bath."

"What about my dress and Snowy's tail?"

"It doesn't matter. You're both still beautiful to me, and you were a gift from my Grandma which makes you even more special."

I looked at Keelee. The Weejum sat on his heels and was unusually silent. He stoked his chin with his fingers.

"I'm so happy Keelee. I can't thank you enough. Why aren't you smiling?"

Keelee stood and took my hand. "I think my people can fix your toys. Want to try?"

"Oh, Yes."

"We have to hurry. The sun will be setting soon in my world. That means it's almost morning in yours."

"Okay, but what should I do?" My excitement made it

hard for me to think.

"Close your eyes and picture the storage hut you saw in my village. If you want to go there bad enough, you will."

I squeezed my eyelids together and thought of the piles of toys. Broken cars, Barbie clothes, and wagons without wheels filled my head. A bright light flashed making me jump. I opened my eyes and streams of light shown through the windows above. Stacks of playthings that had been abandoned by their owners surrounded me.

"Well it's about time you two got here." A Weejum with long, blonde braids stood with her hands on her hips. "Let me see my patients."

Keelee wore a lopsided grin. "Give Melanie and Snowy to Amro."

I handed the doll and the kitten to the female Weejum. Amro wore a white coat like my doctor at home, but Amro's had purple polka dots all over it.

"They sure are messy." The doctor, at least that's what I thought she was, set the toys on the floor. "Wait outside and I'll see what I can do." Amro clapped her hands and pointed to the door.

Keelee and I obeyed orders. We sat on the ground in the shade of a tall willow with our backs resting against the tree's trunk. In a few minutes a white kitten pranced from the

Melanie and Snowy

warehouse tail held high. He made a soft meow and ran in circles making the pink flowers and ribbons around his neck flutter in the breeze he created.

"Wow! You're like brand new, Snowy." I clasped my hands in front of my chest making a steeple.

Trumpets sounded and the building's doors opened again. A red carpet rolled out toward us. Bells tinkled as a beautiful girl stepped outside. She held her head high as she turned in a circle, making her dress swirl. I clapped so hard my palms hurt.

"Melanie, I can't believe how wonderful you look. Better than when I opened your box at my birthday party."

She smiled. "Thank you so much, Jaden, Keelee, and Amro."

"It's getting dark. You'd all better get home before the sun sets," Keelee said.

I scooped up my toys and ran behind the Weejum as he dashed to the other side of his village and through the woods. The door with the jewels glittered in front of us.

I turned to Keelee. "Thank you, my friend. I'll never forget you. Will I ever see you again?"

"Only if you want to."

"I do."

"When I need help finding lost things can I count on you?"

"You know you can." I reached for his hand and gave it a tight squeeze.

A bell began to ring like one in a church steeple. Dong, dong... I opened the door. Twinkle lights greeted me. I stepped onto the path then looked back one last time. The Weejum was gone. Turning my face to the lights, I began walking. Happiness filled my chest. The portal wasn't scary this time. I was going home and precious Melanie and Snowy were with me.

***

About the Author

Mary Ann Bator-Gray lives on Amelia Island, Florida with her wonderful husband and three cats. She enjoys writing and walking the beach, but loves the time she spends at Cats Angels, caring for the many other felines until someone gives them a forever home.

There will be more JADEN AND THE WEEJUM adventures since the female felines at the adoption center are meowing and hissing to have their turn. You can visit them at their website, www.catsangels.com.

During the time of this writing, Slinky and DT found a forever home. Big Blackie, and Shakespeare are still waiting.

Hanging Out at Cats Angels SPCA

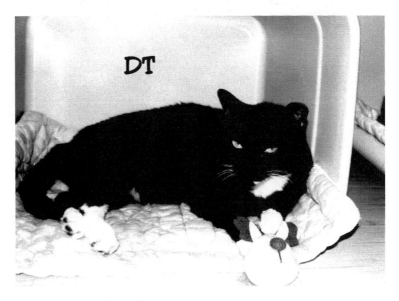

Photo by Evelyn C. McDonald

Photo by Mary Ann Bator-Gray

Photo by Evelyn C. McDonald

Photo by Mary Ann Bator-Gray